STORIES FROM THE ODYSSEY

TOLD TO THE CHILDREN BY
JEANIE LANG

WITH PICTURES BY
W. HEATH ROBINSON

Sandycroft Publishing

Stories from the Odyssey

Told to the Children

By Jeanie Lang

Illustrated by W. Heath Robinson

First published 1906

This edition ©2014

Sandycroft Publishing

http://sandycroftpublishing.com

CONTENTS

LIST OF PICTURES

To My Three Godsons
Geoffrey, Ian, and Tom

About This Book

Almost a thousand years before the Romans came to Britain, while our own forefathers stained themselves blue with woad instead of wearing clothes, and when wild boars and stags and wolves and fierce wild cattle fed where our towns now stand, the people of Greece were singing songs that have been handed down to us even to this day.

The songs were really stories, and these stories were so exciting and so beautiful that men and women and boys and girls alike listened to them with eagerness.

One of those who sang was named Homer. Of him we know little, and are not sure of the little that we know. Some say he was poor and a beggar, and that it was only after he was dead that people found out how great he was.

The stories of his that we know best are called the *The Iliad* and *The Odyssey*. Someday you will read them for yourselves in the Greek in which he told them. You will then know what a writer, who was born in Scotland more than two thousand years after Homer lived, meant when he spoke of

"The surge and thunder of the Odyssey."

And when you read in Greek those wonderful tales of brave men and brave deeds, you will be glad that you have learned to understand the language that Odysseus and the other heroes spoke to each other in days when the world was young.

JEANIE LANG.

And dream idle, happy daydreams that never ended.

Chapter I
How Odysseus Left Troyland and Sailed for His Kingdom Past the Land of the Lotus Eaters

In the days of long ago there reigned over Ithaca, a rugged little island in the sea to the west of Greece, a king whose name was Odysseus. Odysseus feared no man. Stronger and braver than other men was he, wiser, and more full of clever devices. Far and wide he was known as Odysseus of the many counsels. Wise, also, was his queen, Penelope, and she was as fair as she was wise, and as good as she was fair.

While their only child, a boy named Telemachus, was still a baby, there was a very great war in Troyland, a country far across the sea.

The brother of the overlord of all Greece besieged Troy, and the kings and princes of his land came to help him. Many came from afar, but none from a more distant kingdom than Odysseus. Wife and child and old father he left behind him, and sailed away with his black-prowed ships to fight in Troyland.

For ten years the siege of Troy went on, and of the heroes who fought there, none was braver than Odysseus. Clad as a beggar he went into the city and found out much to help the Greek armies. With his long sword he fought his way out again, and left many of the men of Troy lying dead behind him. And many other brave feats did Odysseus do.

After long years of fighting, Troy at last was taken. With much rich plunder the besiegers sailed homewards, and Odysseus set sail for his rocky island, with its great mountain, and its forests of trembling leaves. Of gladness and of longing his heart was full. With a great love he loved his fair wife and little son and old father, and his little kingdom by the sea was very dear to him.

"I can see nought beside sweeter than a man's own country," he said. Very soon he hoped to see his dear land again, but many a long and weary day was to pass ere Odysseus came home.

Odysseus was a warrior, and always he would choose to fight rather than to be at peace.

As he sailed on his homeward way, winds drove his ships near the shore. He and his company landed, sacked the nearest city, and slew the people. Much rich plunder they took, but ere they could return to their ships, a host of people came from inland. In the early morning, thick as leaves and flowers in the spring they came, and fell upon Odysseus and his men.

All day they fought, but as the sun went down the people of the land won the fight. Back to their ships went Odysseus and his men. Out of each ship, were six men slain.

While they were yet sad at heart and weary from the fight, a terrible tempest arose.

Land and sea were blotted out, the ships were driven headlong, and their sails were torn to shreds by the might of the storm. For two days and two nights the ships were at the mercy of the tempest. At dawn on the third day, the storm passed away, and Odysseus and his men set up their masts and hoisted their white sails, and drove homeward before the wind.

So he would have come safely to his own country, but a strong current and a fierce north wind swept the ships from their course. For nine days were they driven far from their homeland, across the deep sea.

On the tenth day they reached the Land of the Lotus Eaters. The dwellers in that land fed on the honey-sweet fruit of the lotus flower. Those who ate of the lotus ceased to remember that there was a past or a future.

All duties they forgot, and all sadness. All day long they would sit and dream and dream idle, happy dreams that never ended.

Here Odysseus and his men landed and drew water. Three of his warriors Odysseus sent into the country to see what manner of men dwelt there.

To them the Lotus Eaters gave their honey-sweet food, and no sooner had each man eaten than he had no wish ever to return to the ships. He longed for ever to stay in that pleasant land, eating the lotus fruit, and dreaming the happy hours away.

Back to the ships Odysseus dragged the unwilling men, weeping that they must leave so much joy behind. Beneath the benches of his ship he tightly bound them, and swiftly he made his ships sail from the shore, lest yet others of his company might eat of the lotus and forget their homes and their kindred.

Soon they had all embarked, and, with heavy hearts, the men of Ithaca smote the grey sea-water with their long oars, and sped away from the land of forgetfulness and of sweet daydreams.

Chapter II
How Odysseus Came to the Land of the Cyclôpes, and His Adventures There

On and on across the waves sailed the dark-prowed ships of Odysseus, until again they came to land. It was the Land of the Cyclôpes, a savage and lawless people, who never planted, nor ploughed, nor sowed, and whose fields yet gave them rich harvests of wheat and of barley, and vines with heavy clusters of grapes. In deep caves, high up on the hills, these people dwelt, and each man ruled his own wife and children, but himself knew no ruler.

Outside the harbour of the Land of the Cyclôpes lay a thickly wooded island. No hunters went there, for the Cyclôpes owned neither ships nor boats, so that many goats roamed unharmed through the woods and cropped the fresh green grass.

It was a green and pleasant land. Rich meadows stretched down to the sea, the vines grew strong and fruitful, and there was a fair harbour where ships might be run right on to the beach. At the head of the harbour was a well of clear water flowing out of a cave, and with poplars growing around it. Thither Odysseus directed his ships. It was dark night, with no moon to guide, and mist lay deep on either side, yet they passed the breakers and rolling surf without knowing it, and anchored safely on the beach.

All night they slept, and when rosy dawn came they explored the island and slew with their bows and long spears many of the wild goats of the woods.

All the livelong day Odysseus and his men sat and feasted. As they ate and drank, they looked across the water at the Land of the Cyclôpes, where the smoke of wood fires curled up to the sky, and from whence they could hear the sound of men's voices and the bleating of sheep and goats. When darkness fell, they lay down to sleep on the sea-beach, and when morning dawned Odysseus called his men together and said to them: "Stay here, all the rest of you, my dear companions, but I will go with my own ship and my ship's company and see what kind of men are those who dwell in this land across the harbour."

So saying, he climbed into his ship, and his men rowed him across to the Land of the Cyclôpes. When they were near the shore they saw a great cave by the sea. It was roofed in with green laurel boughs and seemed to be meant for a fold to shelter sheep and goats. Round about it a high outer wall was firmly built with stones, and with tall and leafy pines and oak trees.

In this cave, all alone with his flocks and herds, dwelt a huge and hideous one-eyed giant.

Polyphemus was his name, and his father was Poseidon, god of the sea.

Taking twelve of his best men with him, Odysseus left the others to guard the ship and sallied forth to the giant's cave. With him he carried a goatskin full of precious wine, dark red, and sweet and strong, and a large sack of corn.

Soon they came to the cave, but Polyphemus was not there. He had taken of his flocks to graze in the green meadows, leaving behind him in the cave folds full of lambs and kids. The walls of the cave were lined with cheeses, and there were great pans full of whey, and giant bowls full of milk.

"Let us first of all take the cheeses," said the men of Odysseus to their king, "and carry them to the ships. Then let us return and drive all the kids and lambs from their folds down to the shore, and sail with them in our swift ships homeward over the sea."

But Odysseus would not listen to what they said. He was too great-hearted to steal into the cave like a thief and take away the giant's goods without first seeing whether Polyphemus might not treat him as a friend, receiving from him the corn and wine he had brought, and giving him gifts in return.

So they kindled a fire, and dined on some of the cheeses, and sat waiting for the giant to return.

Towards evening he came, driving his flocks before him, and carrying on his back a huge load of firewood, which he cast down on the floor with such a thunderous noise that Odysseus and his men fled in fear and hid themselves in the darkest corners of the cave. When he had driven his sheep inside, Polyphemus lifted from the ground a rock so huge that two-and-twenty four-wheeled wagons could not have borne it, and with it blocked the doorway. Then, sitting down, he milked the ewes and bleating goats, and placed the lambs and kids each beside its own mother.

Half of the milk he curdled and placed in wicker baskets to make into cheeses, and the other half he left in great pails to drink when he should have supper. When all this was done, he kindled a fire, and when the flames had lit up the dark-walled cave he spied Odysseus and his men.

"Strangers, who are ye?" he asked, in his great, rumbling voice. "Whence sail ye over the watery ways? Are ye merchants? or are ye sea-robbers who rove over the sea, risking your own lives and bringing evil to other men?"

The sound of the giant's voice, and his hideous face filled the hearts of the men with terror, but Odysseus made answer: "From Troy we come, seeking our home, but driven hither by winds and waves. Men of Agamemnon, the renowned and most mightily victorious Greek general, are we, yet to thee we come and humbly beg for friendship."

At this the giant, who had nothing but cruelty in his heart, mocked at Odysseus. "Thou art a fool," said he, "and I shall not spare either thee or thy company. But tell me where thou didst leave thy good ship? Was it near here, or at the far end of the island?"

But Odysseus of the many counsels knew that the giant asked the question only to bring evil on the men who stayed by the ship, and so he answered: "My ship was broken in pieces by the storm and cast up on the rocks on the shore, but I, with these my men, escaped from death."

Not one word said Polyphemus in reply, but sprang up, clutched hold of two of the men, and dashed their brains out on the stone floor. Then he cut them up, and made ready his supper, eating the two men, bones and all, as if he had been a starving lion, and taking great draughts of the milk from the giant pails. When his meal was done, he stretched himself on the ground beside his sheep and goats, and slept.

In helpless horror Odysseus and his men had watched the dreadful sight, but when the monster slept they began to make plans for their escape. At first Odysseus thought it might be best to take his sharp sword and stab Polyphemus in the breast. But then he knew that even were he thus to slay the giant, he and his men must die. For strength was not left them to roll away the rock from the cave's mouth, and so they must perish like rats in a trap. All night they thought what they should do, but could think of nought that would avail, and so they could only moan in their bitterness of heart and wait for the dawn.

When dawn's rosy fingers touched the sky, Polyphemus awoke. He kindled a fire, and milked his flocks, and gave each ewe her lamb. When this work was done he snatched yet other two men, dashed their brains out, and made of them his morning meal. After the meal, he lifted the stone from the door, drove the flocks out, and set the stone back again. Then, with a loud shout, he turned his sheep and goats towards the hills and left Odysseus and his remaining eight men imprisoned in the cave, plotting and planning how to get away, and how to avenge the death of their comrades.

At last Odysseus thought of a plan. By the sheepfold there lay a huge club of green olive wood that Polyphemus had cut and was keeping until it should be dry enough to use as a staff. So huge was it that Odysseus and his men likened it to the mast of a great merchant vessel. From this club Odysseus cut a large piece and gave it to his men to fine down and make even. While they did this, Odysseus himself sharpened it to a point and hardened the point in the fire. When it was ready, they hid it amongst the rubbish on the floor of the cave. Then Odysseus made his men draw lots who should help him to lift this bar and drive it into the eye of the giant as he slept, and the lot fell upon the four men that Odysseus would himself have chosen.

In the evening Polyphemus came down from the hills with his flocks and drove them all inside the cave. Then he lifted the great doorstone and blocked the doorway, milked the ewes and goats, and gave each lamb and kid to its mother. This done, he seized other two of the men, dashed out their brains, and made ready his supper.

From the shadows of the cave Odysseus now stepped forward, bearing in his hands an ivy bowl, full of the dark red wine.

"Drink wine after thy feast of men's flesh," said Odysseus, "and see what manner of drink this was that our ship held."

Polyphemus grasped the bowl, gulped down the strong wine, and smacked his great lips over its sweetness.

"Give me more," he cried, "and tell me thy name straightway, that I may give thee a gift. Mighty clusters of grapes do the vines of our land bear for us, but this is a rill of very nectar and ambrosia."

Again Odysseus gave him the bowl full of wine, and yet again, until the strong wine went to the giant's head and made him stupid.

Then said Odysseus: "Thou didst ask me my name, and didst say that thou wouldst give me a gift. Noman is my name, and Noman they call me, my father and mother and all my fellows."

Then answered the giant out of his pitiless heart: "I will eat thy fellows first, Noman, and thee the last of all. That shall be thy gift."

Soon the wine made him so sleepy that he sank backwards with his great face upturned and fell fast asleep.

As soon as the giant slept, Odysseus thrust into the fire the stake he had prepared, and made it red hot, all the while speaking cheeringly and comfortingly to his men. When it was so hot that the wood, green though it was, began to blaze, they drew it out and thrust it into the giant's eye. Round and round they whirled the fiery pike, as a man bores a hole in a plank, until the blood gushed out, and the eye frizzled and hissed, and the flames singed and burned the eyelids, and the eye was burned out. With a great and terrible cry the giant sprang to his feet, and Odysseus and the others fled from before him. From his eye he dragged the blazing pike, all dripping with his blood, and dashed it to the ground. Then, maddened with pain, he called with a great and terrible cry on the other Cyclôpes, who dwelt in their caves on the hilltops round which the wind swept. The giants, hearing his horrid yells, rushed to help him.

"What ails thee, Polyphemus?" they asked. "Why dost thou cry aloud in the night and awake us from our sleep? Surely no one stealeth thy flocks? None slayeth thee by force or by craft."

From the other side of the great stone moaned Polyphemus: "Noman is slaying me by craft." Then the Cyclôpes said: "If no man is hurting thee, then indeed it must be a sickness that makes thee cry so loud, and this thou must bear, for we cannot help."

With that they strode away from the cave and left the blind giant groaning and raging with pain. Groping with his hands, he found the great stone that blocked the door, lifted it away, and sat himself down in the mouth of the cave, with his arms stretched out, hoping to catch Odysseus and his men if they should try to escape. Sitting there, he fell asleep, and, as soon as he slept, Odysseus planned and plotted how best to win freedom.

The rams of the giant's flocks were great strong beasts, with fleeces thick and woolly, and as dark as the violet. With twisted slips of willow Odysseus lashed every three of them together, and under the middle ram of each three he bound one of his men. For himself he kept the best ram of the flock, young and strong, and with a fleece wonder fully thick and shaggy. Underneath this ram Odysseus curled himself, and clung, face upwards, firmly grasping the wool with his hands. In this wise did he and his men wait patiently for the dawn.

When rosy dawn came, the ewes in the pens bleated to be milked, and the rams hastened out to the hills and green meadows. As each sheep passed him, Polyphemus felt along its back, but never guessed that the six remaining men of Odysseus were bound beneath the thick-fleeced rams.

Last of all came the young ram to which Odysseus clung, moving slowly, for his fleece was heavy, and Odysseus whom he bore was heavier still. On the ram's back Polyphemus laid his great hands. "Dear ram," said he, "once wert thou the very first to lead the flocks from the cave, the first to nibble the tender buds of the pasture, the first to find out the running streams, and the first to come home when evening fell. But today thou art the very last to go. Surely thou art sorrowful because the wicked Noman hath destroyed my eye. I would thou couldst speak and tell me where Noman is hidden. Then should I seize him and gladly dash out his brains on the floor of the cave."

Very, very still lay Odysseus while the giant spoke, but the ram slowly walked on past the savage giant, towards the meadows near the sea. Soon it was far enough from the cave for Odysseus to let go his hold and to stand up. Quickly he loosened the bonds of the others, and swiftly then they drove the rams down to the shore where their ship lay. Often they looked round, expecting to see Polyphemus following them, but they safely reached the ship and got a glad welcome from their friends, who rejoiced over them, but would have wept over the men that the cannibal giant had slain.

"There is no time to weep," said Odysseus, and he made his men hasten on board the ship, driving the sheep before them.

Soon they were all on board, and the grey sea-water was rushing off their oars, as they sailed away from the land of the Cyclôpes.

But before they were out of sight of land, the bold Odysseus lifted up his voice and shouted across the water:

"Hear me, Polyphemus, thou cruel monster! Thine evil deeds were very sure to find thee out. Thou hast been punished because thou hadst no shame to eat the strangers who came to thee as thy guests!"

The voice of Odysseus rang across the waves, and reached Polyphemus as he sat in pain at the mouth of his cave.

In a fury the giant sprang up, broke off the peak of a great hill and cast it into the sea, where it fell just in front of the ship of Odysseus.

So huge a splash did the vast rock give, that the sea heaved up and the backwash of the water drove the ship right to the shore.

Odysseus snatched up a long pole and pushed the ship off once more. Silently he motioned to the men to row hard, and save themselves and their ship from the angry giant.

When they were once more out at sea, Odysseus wished again to mock Polyphemus. In vain his men begged him not to provoke a monster so mighty that he could crush their heads and the timbers of their ship with one cast of a stone.

Once more Odysseus shouted across the water:

"Polyphemus, if anyone shall ask thee who blinded thee, tell them it was Odysseus of Ithaca."

Then moaned the giant:

"Once, long ago, a soothsayer told me that Odysseus should make me blind. But ever I looked for the coming of a great and gallant hero, and now there hath come a poor, feeble, little dwarf, who made me weak with wine before he dared to touch me."

Then he begged Odysseus to come back, and said he would treat him kindly, and told him that he knew that his own father, the god of the sea, would give him his sight again.

"Never more wilt thou have thy sight," mocked Odysseus; "thy father will never heal thee."

Then Polyphemus, stretching out his hands, and looking up with his sightless eye to the starry sky, called aloud to Poseidon, god of the sea, to punish Odysseus.

"If he ever reaches his own country," he cried, "let him come late and in an evil case, with all his own company lost, and in the ship of strangers, and let him find sorrows in his own house." No answer came from Poseidon, but the god of the sea heard his son's prayer.

With all his mighty force Polyphemus then cast at the ship a rock far greater than the first. It all but struck the end of the rudder, but the huge waves that surged up from it bore on the ship, and carried it to the further shore.

"Never more wilt thou have thy sight," mocked Odysseus.

There they found the men with the other ships waiting in sorrow and dread, for they feared that the giants had killed Odysseus and his company. Gladly they drove the rams of Polyphemus on to the land, and there feasted together until the sun went down.

All night they slept on the sea-beach, and at rosy dawn Odysseus called to his men to get into their ships and loose the hawsers.

Soon they had pushed off, and were thrusting their oars into the grey sea-water.

Their hearts were sore, because they had lost six gallant men of their company, yet they were glad as men saved from death.

For as yet not even wise Odysseus knew of the vengeance of Poseidon, the sea-god, that was to follow him and to make him a sad man for ten long, weary years.

Chapter III
How Odysseus Met with Circe

Across the grey seas sailed Odysseus and his men, until they had left the Land of the Cyclôpes far behind. Ere long they came to an island floating in the sea. Round about it was a wall of bronze, and its cliffs ran sheer up from the water.

Here lived Æolus, the keeper of the winds. For a month the ships of Odysseus rested there, and Odysseus and his men feasted with Æolus and his sons and daughters, and were treated as honoured guests.

When Odysseus said he must again sail on his homeward way, Æolus gave him a parting gift. This gift was a great leather bag, inside which Æolus placed all the winds that he ruled, except the wind of the west. Securely he fastened the mouth of the bag with a silver thong and laid it in the hold of the ship in which Odysseus sailed. Then Æolus bade the West Wind blow gently and softly, and carry the ships safely home to Ithaca.

For nine days and nine nights they sailed smoothly on, gently guided by the soft West Wind, until the hills and woods of Ithaca were in sight, and they could see the people tending the beacon fires to drive wild beasts away from their flocks.

When home was so near, Odysseus felt that he need no longer stay awake day and night, tending, with his own hands, the sail, and guiding the ships. He was very weary, and when sleep made his eyes heavy he gave up his place at the sail to another, and lay down and soundly slept.

While he slept his men grumbled together. "Many are the rich treasures Odysseus brings home with him," said they. "He has riches of every kind from Troy, while we who also fought for Greece have nothing. And now Æolus has given him a gift. The leather bag is certainly full of gold and silver."

Thus they talked, till their greed made thieves of them, and they brought up the leather bag from the hold to steal the treasures which they thought were hidden within.

Quickly they loosened the silver thong, and, with a mighty gust, all the winds rushed out, and swept in a hurricane across the waves, driving the ships before them.

When they saw their own homeland fading away into a little blue speck on the windswept sea, the men of Odysseus wept for their own folly. The sound of their weeping and the roar of the terrible gale awoke Odysseus.

When he knew what had befallen, his heart failed him, and he longed to throw himself into the waves and put an end to his life. But soon his courage came back, and when the storm drove the ships close to the floating island with its bronze walls, he made his men go ashore to get fresh water, and to eat and drink. When he himself had had bread and wine, he went to the palace of Æolus. Here he found Æolus feasting with his wife and children.

In great surprise at seeing him, Æolus said, "How hast thou come hither, Odysseus? What evil hath hindered thy safe voyage? Surely I gave thee every help to take thee safely to thine own country and thy home?"

Then answered Odysseus: "The evil deeds of my own men have brought me this harm. They set free the winds while I slept."

And he begged Æolus to help him, and to let him sail homeward in safety once more. But Æolus would not listen.

"Get thee hence!" he cried in anger. "A very wicked man must thou be, else this evil could not have befallen thee. I will not help thee. Get thee forth!"

Sadder and more heavy at heart than when they landed, Odysseus and his men once more embarked in their ships and left the island. The winds blew fiercely against them, and soon they were utterly worn out and heartsick with toiling at their long, heavy oars.

For six nights and days they struggled on. On the seventh day they reached an island where lived a race of giants. Thankfully, after all their toil, the warriors saw before them a fair harbour. Its entrance was narrow, and steep cliffs ran up on either side of it, but its water was smooth as a pond, with never a little wave to ruffle it. Into this haven all the ships were steered, save the ship of Odysseus. His ship he moored outside the harbour, and fastened the hawser to a rock. Then he with some of his men climbed a crag, from which they could look down on the island. No men or oxen were to be seen, but they saw smoke curling up above the trees.

Three of his men Odysseus sent inland to see what manner of people dwelt there. They went along the track beaten by the wheels that brought wood down from the hills into the town, and presently they came near the town from whence had risen the smoke. Just outside they came on a maiden drawing water from a crystal clear spring. She told the men, when they asked, that she was a princess, daughter of the king of the island, and she showed them the way to her father's palace.

Into the palace she led them, and there they found the queen of the island. She was a huge, fat woman, as big as the peak of a mountain. So horrible was her appearance that when they looked at her they felt sick with fear and disgust.

As soon as she saw the three men she called to her husband. At once he rushed in, seized hold of a man, and, like a hungry lion, began to devour him. The other two men fled to the ships, but the cannibal giant raised a great war-cry, and all the other giants hurried out at the sound. They ran to the cliffs, and there broke off huge rocks which they cast at the ships. Smashed like eggshells, the ships sank under the water, and the noise of crashing timbers and the cries of dying men filled the air. Like men spearing fishes the giants seized the men as they floated on the waters of the harbour, and took them home to devour.

While the haven that had seemed so peaceful was full of those terrible sights and sounds, Odysseus drew his sharp sword, cut his hawser, and bade his ship's company row with all their might. With one accord they dashed their oars into the water, and the ship flew forth from the great dark cliffs of the island out to the open sea. But the ship of Odysseus was the only one that escaped. The other ships were lost there, one and all.

Sad at heart were Odysseus and his men because of the friends who were gone, yet they were glad as men saved from a dreadful death.

Ere long they reached another island, where dwelt a great enchantress, Circe of the Golden Tresses.

The ship of Odysseus put into a sheltering haven and Odysseus and his men went ashore. For two days and two nights they lay by the sea-beach, worn out with weariness and sorrow.

When the third day dawned, Odysseus took his spear and sharp sword and climbed to the top of a craggy hill above the harbour.

From thence he could see the blue smoke curling up above the thick woods, in which stood the palace of Circe. Having seen this he turned back to tell his men what he had seen, and as he came down the path from the hilltop, there came from his pasture in the woodland, to drink at the river, a tall, antlered stag. Odysseus watched him, and as he came out of the river he cast his spear at him, and slew him with one blow.

Then he made a rope of twisted slips of willow, and with it slung the great beast across his back. Walking heavily under his load, he carried the stag to where his ship's company, sad and worn, lay by the sea.

"Take heart, my friends," said he, "we are not yet going to die. Look at the food I have brought, and let us eat and drink."

The men roused themselves to gaze with wonder and delight at the noble stag which Odysseus had cast down on the sea-beach. They prepared a meal of its flesh, and all day they feasted on it and on the sweet wine from their ship. When darkness fell, they lay down to sleep by the sea, and slept until rosy dawn.

When Odysseus awoke, he said to his men:

"Hear my words, my friends. We know not where the sun rises nor where it sets, and all I know of this land is what I saw yesterday from the hill I climbed. All round it lies the sea, and from the thick woods in its midst I saw the smoke curling upwards. So, all round us, we have sea and skies, and a land we do not know."

When the men heard this, they sobbed aloud, for the terrors they had endured had robbed them of their courage.

But Odysseus was brave as before. He divided his men into two companies. One company he himself commanded. His kinsman, Eurylochus, commanded the other. They then drew lots who should explore the island. The lot fell to Eurylochus, and he set out with two-and-twenty men.

In the thick of the forest Eurylochus found the palace of Circe, built of polished stone. A great cleared space lay in front of the palace, and backwards and forwards in this clearing roamed mountain-bred wolves and tawny lions, whom Circe herself had bewitched.

Like dogs that fawn on their master when he comes home, these wild beasts fawned on Eurylochus and his men, wagging their long tails and jumping up on them. At the outer door of the palace the men stood, frightened at these strange and terrible creatures, and from within they heard a silvery voice singing a song so sweet that it stole men's hearts away. It was Circe who sang, singing as she weaved a web of wonderful beauty.

Then the man who of all the men of Odysseus was the one most dear to him, said to the others, "Let us cry aloud to this woman who is weaving, and who sings so sweet a song."

So they called to her, and Circe came forth and opened the shining doors, and, shedding the beauty of her wonderful face on them, she gently bade them enter. Heedlessly they followed her, all but Eurylochus, who, remembering the giant's fair daughter, feared she might betray them.

Into her palace hall she led them, and made them sit on the high seats there. Then she gave them cheese, and barley-meal, and fragrant yellow honey and rich wine, and with their food and wine she mixed harmful drugs that made them utterly forget their own country. Then she smote them with her magic wand, and in one moment they were turned into swine. Four-footed, bristly, and snouted were they, and yet with their own minds inside their ugly bodies, and she penned them into pig-sties, and flung them acorns and other food fit only for pigs.

Long and fearfully Eurylochus waited outside the door of the palace, but when his companions did not return he went back to the ship.

At first he was so full of grief that he could not speak a word, nor tell his story. At length he was able to tell what had befallen. When Odysseus heard how his men had entered the palace but never returned, he flung over his shoulder his silver-studded sword with its great blade of bronze, slung on his bow, and bade Eurylochus lead him by the way he had come.

But, clinging to his knees, Eurylochus in great fear begged Odysseus to leave him behind.

"I know that thou thyself shalt return no more," he said, "nor bring back any one of thy men."

"Stay here, then, by the ship, eating and drinking," said Odysseus scornfully. "As for me, I go."

All alone he went up from the seashore, through the green woods to the enchanted palace.

As he drew near, a fair lad bearing a golden wand came to meet him. Hermes was his name, and he was the messenger of the gods.

17

In one moment they were turned into swine.

Taking Odysseus by the hand, he gently told him how Circe had bewitched his men and turned them into swine, and how Circe would try to serve Odysseus in the same way that she had served them. She would give him food mixed with evil drugs, and when he had eaten she would smite him with her magic wand, and send him grunting to a sty.

"But I will save thee," said Hermes, "and prevent Circe from doing thee harm."

With that he gave Odysseus a strange plant, black at the root, but with a flower as white as milk. Moly, he called it, and it was so hard to dig that mere men were scarcely able to dig it. He told Odysseus that if he carried the Moly with him, Circe would not be able to enchant him.

"When Circe smites thee with her long wand," said he, "even then draw thy sharp sword and spring on her as if thou wouldst slay her. Then she will shrink away in fear, and ever after she will treat thee kindly. Only thou must make her promise that she will plan no more mischief against thee." Then Hermes of the golden wand went away through the trees, and Odysseus held on his way to the palace.

At the gates of the palace he stood and called aloud. Soon the shining doors were swung open, and beautiful, wicked Circe, with her golden hair hanging round her false, fair face, came and led him in.

She made him sit on a carved chair, studded with silver, and brought him a golden cup full of her drugged wine.

When he had drunk of it, she smote him with her wand, and said, "Go thy way now to the sty, and lie there with the rest of thy company." At that Odysseus did as Hermes had bidden, and, drawing his sharp sword, he rushed at Circe as if to slay her.

With a great cry, Circe slipped to the ground and clasped Odysseus round the knees.

"There is no man save one who is great enough to be proof against the charm which thou hast drunk," she cried. "Truly thou must be Odysseus of whom Hermes of the golden wand hath ofttimes told me. From Troy, in thy swift black ship, he said thou wouldst come. Sheathe thy sword, I pray thee, Odysseus, and let us be at peace."

Then said Odysseus: "How canst thou bid me be at peace with thee, Circe, when thou by thy wicked magic hast turned my men into swine? How can I trust thee?"

19

Then Circe solemnly promised to do Odysseus no harm, and to let him return in safety to his home.

Quickly her servants spread fair linen on the floor, and covered the chairs with covers of rich purple. Tables of silver they drew up near the chairs, and on them placed golden dishes full of tempting food, and silver bowls and golden cups full of sweet wine. They also made ready a warm bath for Odysseus, and when he had bathed they brought him a fair mantle and tunic. Then Circe made him sit on a beautiful chair, inlaid with silver, and with a footstool at his feet. A maid brought water in a golden ewer and poured it into a silver basin for him to wash his hands, and served him with every kind of dainty.

But Odysseus could not eat. His mind was full of care, and he thought sadly of his friends who were even then penned like swine in a sty.

"Why art thou so sad and silent, Odysseus?" asked Circe. "Why wilt thou not eat? Art thou afraid that I will deceive thee and harm thee? Nay, thou hast no cause for fear, for I have sworn I will do thee no hurt."

Odysseus answered: "How can I be happy, and eat and drink, when I have not yet freed my dear friends? If thou wilt set them free, then indeed shall I know that thou wilt keep the promise thou hast made."

Then Circe went through the great hall to the sty where the bewitched men were imprisoned. She opened the doors of the sty and waved her wand, and when the swine came out she touched each one with a charm that made its bristles and pig's body and face disappear. And they became men again, and looked even handsomer and stronger than before.

When they saw Odysseus, they ran to him and took his hands, and wept for joy. And even Circe's hard heart was melted at their gladness, and tears came into her eyes.

Then Circe asked Odysseus to bring up his men from the seashore, that they might all feast together. Down by the ship he found them sorrowing, because they feared they should see him no more. So dearly did they love Odysseus that they were as glad when they saw him safe and well, as they would have been had they themselves safely returned to their own homeland. When he told them to draw the ship on shore, and hide their goods in the sea-caves, and come and feast in Circe's palace, they gladly obeyed.

Eurylochus alone, who did not wish to go, tried to prevent the others from going. "Wretched men that we are!" he cried, "Odysseus is always foolhardy, and always leading us into danger. It was he who put us into the power of the Cyclôpes, and now he leads us to the enchantress, Circe, who will surely turn us all into swine, or wolves or lions to guard her palace."

So angry was Odysseus at these words, that he laid his hand on his sword, and would have cut off the head of Eurylochus. But the other men of his company pleaded for mercy for him.

"Leave Eurylochus here to guard the ship," said they, "but lead us to the palace of Circe."

And Eurylochus, ashamed, did not stay by the ship, but went with the others.

When they reached the palace, Circe provided warm baths and rich clothes for the tired and hungry men, and made them a great feast.

And when Odysseus saw them all safe and happy, he, too, was happy, and ate of the banquet that Circe had made for him.

For a whole year Odysseus and his men stayed in the palace, feasting and resting. But when a year was gone, and the long summer days had returned once more, his men came to Odysseus and said:

"Surely it is high time for us to think of our own homes, and our own dear land. Are we to stay here evermore?"

That night Odysseus said to Circe:

"Circe, thou didst promise to let me return to my own country. My men and I long with a great homesickness to see our land again. Wilt thou let us go?"

Said Circe: "Thou shalt stay no longer in my house against thy will, Odysseus."

So when some days had passed, and when Circe had told Odysseus of many dangers he would meet on his homeward voyage, and warned him how best to escape from them, Odysseus said farewell to the sorceress.

"If thou or thy men do what I have warned them not to do," she said, "ruin will come upon thy ship, and on thy men. And thou, Odysseus, even though thou shouldest thyself escape, shalt return to Ithaca late, and in evil plight, and with the loss of all thy company."

When dawn was turning the tops of the trees on the enchanted island into gold, Odysseus and his men got on board their ship. They thrust their oars deep into the grey sea-water, but soon they ceased to row, for Circe sent a kindly wind to fill the sails and carry Odysseus safely home.

As the ship flew swiftly through the water, like a bird that swims through the waves, Circe of the golden hair walked up from the shore, through the green woods, to the enchanted palace.

Sad was her heart at the parting, and mayhap she grieved for the evil she had wrought.

Chapter IV
How Odysseus Escaped from the Sirens, and How His Ship was Wrecked

In an island in the blue sea through which the ship of Odysseus would cut its homeward way, lived some beautiful mermaids called Sirens. Even more beautiful than the Sirens' faces were their lovely voices.

In the flowery meadows of their island they sat singing their sweet songs, and the sailors whose ships were passing could not forbear to go on shore, and there were they slain by the wicked mermaids. All around them in the meadows where the Sirens sat were the bones of the men they had slain. But these the foolish sailors did not see. They only saw the bright-coloured flowers, and the mermaids' lovely faces and long, golden hair. And the songs, whose melody mingled with the sound of the little white-fringed waves that swished up on the yellow sand, stole their hearts away.

Against these mermaids Circe had warned Odysseus, and he repeated her warnings to his men.

A gentle breeze sped the ship of Odysseus quickly on its way, but as they neared the island the sirens by their spells sent a dead calm and the waves were lulled to sleep. Not a breath of air filled the white sails, so the men drew them in and stowed them in the hold, and rowed with their long oars until the green water grew white.

Meantime Odysseus, as Circe had bidden him, took a great piece of wax, cut it in pieces with his sharp sword, and quickly moulded it with his strong hands.

Soon the wax grew warm and soft, and with it he then filled the ears of each one of his men. He himself used no wax, but made his company bind him hand and foot upright to the mast.

"If, when I hear the voices of the mermaidens, I struggle and sign to thee to set me free, then bind me with yet more bonds," said Odysseus.

"Drive thy ship swiftly past the island," Circe had said. So the men bent to their oars and smote the grey sea-water.

23

In the meadows where the sirens sat were the bones of the men they had slain.

Past the island drove the dark-prowed ship, but the sirens seeing it began their sweet song. "Come hither, come hither, brave Odysseus," they sang. "Here stay thy black ship and listen to our song. No one hath ever passed this way in his ship till he hath heard from our lips the music that is sweet as honeycomb, and hath had joy of it, and gone on his way the wiser. All things are known to us. We will sing to thee of thy great fights and victories in Troyland. We shall sing of all the things that shall be hereafter. Come hither, come hither, Odysseus!"

So sweet and so full of magic were their voices, that when Odysseus had heard their song, and seen them smilingly beckoning to him from amongst the flowers, he tried to make his men unbind him.

Frowning and nodding, he signed to them to set him free, but Eurylochus and another rose from their places and bound him yet more tightly to the mast. The men themselves, deafened by the wax, heard none of the song and wished not to stop, but stoutly rowed onward.

When the island was left behind, and Odysseus no longer heard the silvery voices, but only the moan of the waves far away and the rush of the water off the oars, the men took the wax from their ears and unbound their captain.

Soon they heard a sound far different from the song of the Sirens.

"Thou shalt pass the Wandering Rocks," Circe had said. "There great and furious waves dash themselves upon the rugged cliffs. Even the wild birds cannot fly past them, but are beaten down by the force of the spray. The whirlpool beside them tosses up and churns about continually the planks of the ships and the bodies of the men it has destroyed."

When Odysseus heard the thunder of the sea and saw mighty waves rushing and roaring against the rocks, and the smoke of the spray dashing up into the sky, he knew that they had reached the Wandering Rocks.

So terrible were the sights and sounds that the men let the oars slip from their hands, and stared and listened in horror.

But Odysseus paced along the ship and spoke cheering words to them.

"This is no greater woe," he said, "than what we bore when we were penned into his cave by the cannibal giant. From that cave we escaped, and someday I think we shall be able also to talk of this adventure. Only do now as I say. Ye oarsmen, drive thine oars deep and strongly into the angry surf and row with all thy might. And thou at the helm, keep the ship well away from the great waves and the spray, and hug the rocks. So may we escape even from this peril."

But the Wandering Rocks were not the only danger there for the ship. Beyond them were yet two huge rocks between which the sea swept.

One of these, a dark and dreadful peak, ran straight up to the sky. Over it hung a black cloud even in the fairest summer weather. No mortal could climb it, not even if he had twenty hands and feet, for it was smooth and slippery as glass. In this cliff was a dark cave in which lived a horrible monster called Scylla. All day and all night she yelped like a savage dog. She had twelve feet and six heads, each head with three rows of sharp teeth. Up to her waist she was hidden in the darkness of the cave. Her six heads, with their long necks, constantly swooped and craned and darted out like great fierce birds, and seized all the dolphins and sea-dogs, and big fishes that came within reach. When ships passed near her cave Scylla had a feast, for with each head she would seize a sailor and crunch him up with her horrid teeth.

Opposite this cliff was another rock, on which grew a great fig-tree in full leaf. Beneath it dwelt another monster, Charybdis. Three times a day did Charybdis suck down the salt sea-water, and three times a day did she force it out again from her black cave under the sea. If a ship passed while she sucked, it was drawn down into the dreadful gulf where the monster lived, and only its fragments were tossed up in the boiling surf.

Odysseus spoke to his men of the Wandering Rocks, but he dared not tell them of Scylla and Charybdis lest, in their terror, they should cease to row, and hide themselves in the hold.

When Circe warned him of the dangers he would meet, he asked her how he could best escape from Scylla and Charybdis.

"Scylla is no mortal," Circe had said. "She cannot be fought with, and against her there is no defence. Tarry not to put on thine armour and to fight. Drive past her with all thy force." But when the noise of the furious sea, and the hideous yelping of Scylla were in his ears, Odysseus forgot what Circe had said. He hated Scylla so much that he longed to slay her. Hastily he put on his shining armour and caught up two long lances, and stood at the prow, ready to fight with the monster of the rock.

His eyes grew weary with peering into the darkness of the cave from whence he expected her hideous heads to dart, but he saw nothing, and turned away at last to gaze at the black whirlpool of Charybdis.

White-faced with the terror of it the men rowed steadily, while Charybdis gulped down the water and threw it up again in swirling surf and spray that dashed to the tops of the cliffs. Past the Wandering Rocks they rowed their ship in safety. Almost past the black cliff of Scylla they had pulled, almost past the fierce whirlpool, when six monster heads swooped out from the blackness of the cave. In a moment six of the men were seized and borne aloft, struggling in the greedy jaws of Scylla, and crying pitifully to Odysseus for help.

But no help could Odysseus give. The monster had her meal, and evermore Odysseus remembered the sight of the death of his six brave men as the pitifullest thing he had ever seen.

At last, when the rocks were left behind, the ship came to a fair island where grazed the sacred cattle of the god of the Sun.

"Hurt not the cattle on that fair island," Circe had said, "for if thou hurtest them ruin shall come on thy ship and thy men, and even though thou shouldest thyself escape, thou shalt return home in evil plight, with the loss of all thy company."

The lowing of the cattle, as the ship neared the fair island, made Odysseus think of the evils that might come, and he begged his men to row on past the isle.

Then Eurylochus spoke: "Surely thou art made of iron and thy limbs are never weary, Odysseus," he said. "Thy men are worn out, yet instead of letting them land and allowing them to prepare a good supper, thou drivest them on. Thou bidst us row blindly through the black night, and go wandering on the misty deep. In the night blow the winds that wreck ships. How shall we weary men escape if a sudden fierce blast should blow? Let us rather rest here and sup. In the fair morning light we will start again and row homeward across the sea."

The tired men gladly agreed with Eurylochus.

Then said Odysseus: "Promise, then, that none of ye will slay any of the sacred oxen of the Sun, but that ye will be content to eat of the food we have with us."

Straightway they promised, and the ship was anchored in a little harbour near where was a well of sweet water, and soon they had supper ready on the shore.

As darkness fell, they talked much of the dear friends that Scylla had devoured, and, weeping for their loss, they fell asleep.

A great storm raged through the night, but dawn broke rosy and clear. When it was morning they dragged the ship ashore and hid it in a hollow cave.

All that day a strong south wind blew, and every day for a month it never ceased.

And they dared not go afloat again because of the fierceness of the gales.

At first the men had plenty of food and were well content. But presently the food began to fail, and they had to try to catch fish, and to wander in the island and try to kill birds to eat, for hunger gnawed them.

One day when they were all very hungry Odysseus left his men by the sea, and went away to the middle of the island by himself that he might think what to do, and how they might best return home.

But he was so hungry and so tired that he fell asleep while he was thinking, and while he slept Eurylochus made mischief, as was his wont.

"Shall we die of hunger?" he said to the others, "and yet have good food so near us? Let us slay some of the best of these straight-horned cattle, and when we are home at Ithaca let us build a splendid altar to the god of the Sun and give him many rich gifts. But if he should be angry at us for slaying the cattle, and should wreck our ship, far better that we should so die than that we should slowly starve to death on this desert island."

The men quickly did as Eurylochus advised. The finest of the cattle that were feeding near were slain, and soon savoury pieces of their flesh were roasting on spits at the fire which had been kindled.

While they feasted Odysseus awoke and hurried down to the shore. As he drew near, the smell of the roasting flesh met him, and he groaned aloud with horror.

One by one he rebuked his men, but it was too late. The cattle were dead and gone, and the evil could not be mended.

Already the men rued what they had done, for strange and fearful things befell. The skins of the dead beasts were creeping, the flesh bellowed upon the spits as it was being cooked, and a sound as of the lowing of many cattle filled the air.

Yet they hardened their hearts, and for six days their feast went on.

On the seventh day the wind at last ceased to blow heavy gales, and Odysseus and his men launched their ship and hoisted its white sails, and soon had left the island far behind.

When they were out of sight of all land, and saw only sky and sea, a dark cloud appeared over the ship, and the water darkened beneath it.

Then, on a sudden, with a shrill scream, a great tempest burst upon them. The mast snapped before its furious rush and fell with a crash on the pilot, crushing in his head, so that he dropped, like a diver, into the sea.

At that minute a mighty thunderbolt smote the ship, filling it with flame and sulphur, and making it reel over to one side. The men fell from it into the sea, and for one moment Odysseus saw them, like sea-gulls, borne aloft on the great waves round the ship. Then they sank, and he never saw them more.

Still Odysseus paced his ship, till the storm and the sea had smashed her into pieces. Then he lashed the keel and the mast together, and, sitting on it, was driven onward by the furious winds.

All night he was carried swiftly on, and when the sun rose he found that the winds and the waves had carried him close to Scylla and Charybdis.

The black whirlpool of Charybdis gaped to swallow him, but as the piece of wreckage to which he had clung went down into the gulf Odysseus made a mighty leap and seized hold of the fig-tree that grew on the cliff. He held on to it like a bat until Charybdis had cast up again the piece of broken mast.

The moment it appeared Odysseus let himself drop into the sea just beyond it, and, clambering on to it, he rowed hard with his hands. Scylla was not on the outlook, or it would have gone ill with him, but he safely escaped from her and from Charybdis.

For nine days and nights he was tossed by the waves. On the night of the ninth day the mast drifted to the shores of an island, and Odysseus, little life left in him, crawled on to the dry land.

Chapter V
How Odysseus Left the Island of Calypso

Calypso of the braided tresses was a goddess feared by all men. It was to her island that the piece of wreckage to which Odysseus clung drifted on the ninth dark night after his ship was wrecked.

At night the island looked black and gloomy, but at morning light, when Odysseus felt life and strength coming back to him, he saw that it was a beautiful place.

In the sunlight, the grey, cruel sea was violet blue, and violets blue as the sea grew thickly in the green meadows. From the seashore he walked inland until he came to a great cave, and in the cave sat Calypso, the beautiful goddess with the braided hair.

On the hearth a great fire burned, and the fragrance of the burning cedar and sandalwood could be smelt afar off in the island. Calypso, wearing a shining robe and a golden girdle, was weaving with a shuttle of gold and singing as she wove. Round about the cave alders and poplars and sweet-smelling cypresses grew, and in them roosted owls and falcons and chattering sea-crows, and the long-winged, white-plumaged sea-birds. A vine with rich clusters of grapes climbed up the cave, and four fountains of clear water played beside it.

Odysseus knew that Calypso was a goddess that all men feared, but he soon found that he had nothing to fear from her, save that she should keep him in her island forevermore. She tended him gently and lovingly until his weariness and weakness were gone and he was as strong as ever.

But although he lived by the meadows where the violets and wild parsley grew, and had lovely Calypso to give him all that he wished, Odysseus had a sad and heavy heart.

"Stay with me, and thou shalt never grow old and never die," said Calypso.

But a great homesickness was breaking the heart of Odysseus. He would rather have had one more glimpse of his rocky little kingdom across the sea, and then have died, than have lived forever and forever young in the beautiful, flowery island.

Day after day he would go down to the shore and stare with longing eyes across the water. But eight years came and went, and he seemed no nearer escape.

Yet, although he did not know it, the days of the wanderings of Odysseus were soon to end.

It was Poseidon, the god of the sea, who had sent all his troubles to Odysseus, because he had blinded his son, the wicked cannibal giant.

It was the grey-eyed Athene, a goddess who had always been the friend of Odysseus, who helped to bring him home. When she saw him daily sitting by the sea, gazing across the water with great tears rolling down his face, her heart was filled with pity. She knew, too, what troubles his wife and son were having in Ithaca while Odysseus was far away, and at length she went to the gods and begged them to help her to send Odysseus safely back to his kingdom.

Poseidon had gone to a far-distant land, and when the gods knew through what bitter sorrows Odysseus had passed, and how his heart ached to look once again even on the blue smoke curling up above the woods in Ithaca, they took pity on him.

They called Hermes of the golden wand, their fleet-footed messenger. On his feet Hermes bound his golden sandals that never grew old, and that bore him safely and swiftly over wet sea and dry land. In his hand he took his golden wand, with which he could lull people to sleep. Like a sea-bird that chases the fish through the depths of the sea, and dips its white plumage in the rolling breakers, so sped Hermes over the waves.

When he had reached the island of Calypso, he walked through the meadows of violets to the cave. But Odysseus was not there. Down by the rocky shore he sat, looking wistfully over the wide sea, while the tears rolled down his face and dripped on the sand. Calypso was in the cave, weaving with her golden shuttle, and singing a sweet song. Food and wine she gave to Hermes, and when he had eaten and drunk he gave her the message of the gods.

When she heard that the gods commanded her to let Odysseus go safely home, Calypso was very sad.

"Hard and jealous are ye gods," she said. "It was I who saved Odysseus as he clung to the piece of wreckage that drifted in the sea, and guided him safely to my island. Ever since have I been kind to him and have loved him, and now you are taking him away from me. But how can I send him? I have no ships nor men to take him back to Ithaca."

"If thou dost not send him, thou wilt anger all the gods," said Hermes, "and greatly will they punish thee."

Then Hermes sped away across the violet meadows and the violet-blue sea, and Calypso went down to where Odysseus sat on the shore.

"Sorrow no more, poor man," she said, "for now, with all my heart, will I send thee home. Arise, and cut long beams. With thine axe make a wide raft and lay cross planks above for a deck. In it I shall place food and water, and give thee clothing, and send a fair wind, so that thou mayest come safely to thine own country. For such is the will of the gods, who are stronger than I am both to will and to do."

"But surely thou plannest mischief," Odysseus said. "Thou bidst me cross the mighty sea in a little raft. I would not go aboard a raft, unless thou shouldst give me thy promise not to plan secretly my ruin."

Calypso smiled, and gently laid her hand on his shoulder.

"I give my promise," she said. "I am planning for thee as I should plan for myself were I in a like case. My heart is not of iron, Odysseus, but pitiful as thine."

Then she gave him a great, double-edged axe of bronze, with a strong handle of olive-wood, and a polished adze, and led the way to the border of the island, where grew tall trees, alders and poplars and pines. When she had shown him where the tall trees grew, she went home.

Odysseus went gladly and quickly to work. With his axe of bronze he soon had felled twenty great trees and had trimmed and neatly planed them. That done, Calypso brought him other tools, and bolts, and a web of cloth to make sails, and skilfully and well he made his raft. In four days his work was done, and he drew the vessel down with rollers to the sea.

On the fifth day, when Calypso had given him new warm clothes, and had put plenty of corn and wine and water, and many dainties that she knew Odysseus liked, in the raft, she said farewell. She sent a gentle breeze to blow, and Odysseus rejoiced as the wind filled his sails and carried him away from the island. Calypso had told him what stars he must use as his guides, and all her advice he followed, and so in eighteen days he saw land appear.

It was the land of the Phæacians, who were famous sailors, and it looked like a shield lying in the misty sea.

But just when safety and home seemed very near Odysseus, his enemy, Poseidon the sea-god, returned from his wanderings in far-off lands.

When he saw Odysseus peacefully sailing towards the land of the Phæacians, he knew that while he had been away the gods must have changed their minds, and were sending Odysseus safely home.

"Ha!" said the angry god, "Odysseus thinks all his sorrows are over. Even yet I think I can drive him far enough in the path of suffering."

With that he gathered the clouds into great stormy masses, and roused up the waters of the deep. Soon the thick black mist hid both land and sea. He let loose all the fierce storms and wild winds, and made the dark night rush down. The winds fought and clashed together and made the sea swell up into furious billows that rolled onward, mountain high, towards the shore.

Then the heart of Odysseus failed him. "Wretched man that I am," said he, "would that I had met my death fighting in Troyland, and been buried like a brave soldier there."

As he spoke, a mighty wave smote the raft and rushed over it. The helm was torn from his hand, the mast was broken in two, the sail and yard-arm were hurled far away, and Odysseus was swept into the sea.

For long the weight and force of the huge wave kept him under, and his clothes were so heavily clogged with water that they made him sink. But at last he came up, and spat from his mouth the bitter salt water that streamed down his face and head. Even then he did not forget his raft, but made a spring after it in the waves, clutched hold of it, and clambered in again.

Hither and thither the great waves carried it. Like a scrap of thistledown chased before the winds, even so was the raft of Odysseus driven. The south wind would toss it to the north, and again the east wind would cast it to the west to chase.

So pitiful was the sight of brave Odysseus thus tortured by the vengeful god of the sea, that a fair sea-nymph felt sorrow for him.

Rising like a white-winged sea-gull from the waves, she climbed on to the raft and spake to Odysseus.

"The sea-god shall not slay thee," she said. "Do as I tell thee, and thou shalt not die. Cast off these heavy, water-logged clothes, leave the raft to drift, and swim with all thy strength to the land. Take now my veil and wind it round thee. With it on thou shalt be safe, and when thou dost grasp the mainland with thy hands, turn thy head away and let the veil fly back to the sea."

With that she gave him her veil and dived like a bird into the water, and the dark waves closed over her.

But Odysseus believed not in her kindness.

"The gods have made a new plot for my ruin," he thought. "I will not obey this sea-nymph. This shall I do,—as long as the timbers of my raft hold together, here will I stay. But if the storm shall drive the raft in pieces, then shall I swim, for there is nought else to do."

Then the god of the sea stirred up against him a wave more terrible than any that had gone before, and with it smote the raft. Like chaff scattered by a great wind, so were the planks and beams of the raft scattered hither and thither. But Odysseus laid hold on a plank and bestrode it, as he might have ridden a horse. He stript off his wet clothes and wound around him the sea-nymph's veil. Then he dropped from the plank, and swam with all his might.

The god of the sea saw him and scornfully wagged his head.

"Go wandering over the sea, then," he said, "until thou findest help."

Then he lashed his sea-horses, with their flowing white manes, and drove away to his own home far below the sea.

But Athene also saw Odysseus and bade all the winds be still but the swift North Wind. "Blow hard, North Wind," she said, "and break the way before Odysseus till thou hast carried him on to the land of the Phæacians."

For two days and two nights Odysseus was borne onward on the swell of the sea.

When the third day dawned the breeze fell and there was a breathless calm, and he saw the land very near. With his heart near bursting with joy he swam on until he could see the trees on the shore.

Just then a great sound smote his ear, and he knew it was the thunder of the sea against a reef. Soon he saw that on that coast

The nymph rose from the sea and bore the veil away.

there were no harbours, nor any shelter for ships, but only jutting headlands and reefs, and great, rugged crags against which the sea broke thundering and crashing, and surging back in angry foam.

Then thought Odysseus: "At last I have had a sight of the land, but there is no way to escape from the grey waters. If I try to land, the waves will dash my life out on those jagged rocks. If I swim further round the coast and try to find some inlet, then the storm-winds may catch me again and bear me onward far from the land, or the sea-god may send a monster from the shore water to devour me."

But as he was thinking, a great wave bore him to where the breakers thundered on the reef. All his bones would have been broken, and his life dashed from his body, if Athene had not put a thought into his heart. As he was swept in with the rush of the wave, he clutched hold of the rock and clung there till the wave had gone by. But the fierce back-wash rushed on him, and the furious surge tore off his clinging fingers and cast him into the sea. With bleeding hands he sank under the great waves, and might have perished there, had not Athene once again whispered to him. He rose and swam outside the line of breakers, always looking for some inlet, until at length he came to where a fair river joined the sea.

Then Odysseus called aloud to the river and begged it to have pity on him, and to let him at last get safely to the land.

And the river was kind, and made the water smooth, and bore him up in its shining stream until he had reached the shore.

All bruised and swollen was his body, great streams of salt water gushed from his nostrils, but he lay on dry land at last, his breath and speech gone, well-nigh swooning. When he came to himself, he took the sea-nymph's veil and let it fall into the river. Swiftly it swept down the stream, and the nymph rose from the sea, caught it in her hands, and bore it away. Then Odysseus, kneeling down amongst the reeds by the river, kissed the earth for very gladness and thankfulness of heart.

"The river breeze blows shrewd and chill in the morning," he thought, "and the frosty night down here by the river might kill me."

So he climbed up the hillside to a shady wood, and crept under the shelter of two olive-trees that grew so close together that no keen wind, nor sun, nor rain could pierce them.

There he made himself a bed of dry leaves, and lay down and heaped over himself the warm and fragrant covering.

Then Athene sent sleep to close his eyes, and at last warmth and comfort and happy dreams made him forget all the terrible things through which he had passed.

Chapter VI
How Odysseus Met with Nausicaa

In the land of the Phæacians there dwelt no more beautiful, nor any sweeter maiden, than the king's own daughter. Nausicaa was her name, and she was so kind and gentle that everyone loved her.

To the land of the Phæacians the North Wind had driven Odysseus, and while he lay asleep in his bed of leaves under the olive-trees, the goddess Athene went to the room in the palace where Nausicaa slept, and spoke to her in her dreams.

"Someday thou wilt marry, Nausicaa," she said, "and it is time for thee to wash all the fair raiment that is one day to be thine. Tomorrow thou must ask the king, thy father, for mules and for a wagon, and drive from the city to a place where all the rich clothing may be washed and dried."

When morning came Nausicaa remembered her dream, and went to tell her father.

Her mother was sitting spinning yarn of sea-purple stain, and her father was just going to a council meeting.

"Father, dear," said the princess, "couldst thou lend me a high wagon with strong wheels, that I may take all my fair linen to the river to wash. All yours, too, I shall take, so that thou shalt go to the council in linen that is snowy clean, and I know that my five brothers will also be glad if I wash their fine clothing for them."

This she said, for she felt too shy to tell her father what Athene had said about her getting married.

But the king knew well why she asked. "I do not grudge thee mules, nor anything else, my child," he said. "Go, bid the servants prepare a wagon."

The servants quickly got ready the finest wagon that the king had, and harnessed the best of the mules. And Nausicaa's mother filled a basket with all the dainties that she knew her daughter liked best, so that Nausicaa and her maidens might feast together. The fine clothes were piled into the wagon, the basket of food was placed carefully beside them, and Nausicaa climbed in, took the whip and shining reins, and touched the mules. Then with clatter of hoofs they started.

When they were come to the beautiful, clear river, amongst whose reeds Odysseus had knelt the day before, they unharnessed the mules and drove them along the banks of the river to graze where the clover grew rich and fragrant. Then they washed the clothes, working hard and well, and spread them out to dry on the clean pebbles down by the seashore.

Then they bathed, and when they had bathed they took their midday meal by the bank of the rippling river.

When they had finished, the sun had not yet dried the clothes, so Nausicaa and her maidens began to play ball. As they played they sang a song that the girls of that land would always sing as they threw the ball to one another. All the maidens were fair, but Nausicaa of the white arms was the fairest of all.

From hand to hand they threw the ball, growing always the merrier, until, when it was nearly time for them to gather the clothes together and go home, Nausicaa threw it very hard to one of the others. The girl missed the catch. The ball flew into the river, and, as it was swept away to the sea, the princess and all her maidens screamed aloud.

Their cries awoke Odysseus, as he lay asleep in his bed of leaves.

"I must be near the houses of men," he said; "those are the cries of girls at play." With that he crept out from the shelter of the olive-trees.

He had no clothes, for he had thrown them all into the sea before he began his terrible swim for life. But he broke off some leafy branches and held them round him, and walked down to where Nausicaa and her maidens were.

Like a wild man of the woods he looked, and when they saw him coming the girls shrieked and ran away. Some of them hid behind the rocks on the shore, and some ran out to the spits of yellow sand that jutted into the sea.

But although his face was marred with the sea-foam that had crusted on it, and he looked a terrible, fierce, great creature, Nausicaa was too brave to run away.

Shaking she stood there, and watched him as he came forward, and stood still a little way off. Then Odysseus spoke to her, gently and kindly, that he might take away her fear.

He told her of his shipwreck, and begged her to show him the way to the town, and give him some old garment, or any old wrap in which she had brought the linen, so that he might have something besides leaves with which to cover himself.

"I have never seen any maiden half so beautiful as thou art," he said. "Have pity on me, and may the gods grant thee all thy heart's desire."

Then said Nausicaa: "Thou seemest no evil man, stranger, and I will gladly give thee clothing and show thee the way to the town. This is the land of the Phæacians, and my father is the king."

To her maidens then she called:

"Why do ye run away at the sight of a man? Dost thou take him for an enemy? He is only a poor shipwrecked man. Come, give him food and drink, and fetch him clothing."

The maidens came back from their hiding-places, and fetched some of the garments of Nausicaa's brothers which they had brought to wash, and laid them beside Odysseus.

Odysseus gratefully took the clothes away, and went off to the river. There he plunged into the clear water, and washed the salt crust from off his face and limbs and body, and the crusted foam from his hair. Then he put on the beautiful garments that belonged to one of the princes, and walked down to the shore where Nausicaa and her maidens were waiting.

So tall and handsome and strong did Odysseus look, with his hair curling like hyacinth flowers around his head, that Nausicaa said to her maidens: "This man, who seemed to us so dreadful so short a time ago, now looks like a god. I would that my husband, if ever I have one, should be as he."

Then she and her maidens brought him food and wine, and he ate hungrily, for it was many days since he had eaten.

When he had finished, they packed the linen into the wagon, and yoked the mules, and Nausicaa climbed into her place.

"So long as we are passing through the fields," she said to Odysseus, "follow behind with my maidens, and I will lead the way. But when we come near the town with its high walls and towers, and harbours full of ships, the rough sailors will stare and say, 'Hath Nausicaa gone to find herself a husband because she scorns the men of Phæacia who would wed her? Hath she picked up a shipwrecked stranger, or is this one of the gods who has come to make her his wife?' Therefore

Nausicaa and her maidens brought him food and wine.

come not with us, I pray thee, for the sailors to jest at. There is a fair poplar grove near the city, with a meadow lying round it. Sit there until thou thinkest that we have had time to reach the palace. Then seek the palace—any child can show thee the way—and when thou art come to the outer court pass quickly into the room where my mother sits. Thou wilt find her weaving yarn of sea-purple stain by the light of the fire. She will be leaning her head back against a pillar, and her maidens will be standing round her. My father's throne is close to hers, but pass him by, and cast thyself at my mother's knees. If she feels kindly towards thee and is sorry for thee, then my father is sure to help thee to get safely back to thine own land."

Then Nausicaa smote her mules with the whip, and they trotted quickly off, and soon left behind them the silver river with its whispering reeds, and the beach with its yellow sand.

Odysseus and the maidens followed the wagon, and just as the sun was setting they reached the poplar grove in the meadow.

There Odysseus stayed until Nausicaa should have had time to reach the palace. When she got there, she stopped at the gateway, and her brothers came out and lifted down the linen, and unharnessed the mules. Nausicaa went up to her room, and her old nurse kindled a fire for her and got ready her supper.

When Odysseus thought it was time to follow, he went to the city. He marvelled at the great walls and at the many gallant ships in the harbours. But when he reached the king's palace, he wondered still more. Its walls were of brass, so that from without, when the doors stood open, it looked as if the sun or moon were shining within. A frieze of blue ran round the walls. All the doors were made of gold, the doorposts were of silver, the thresholds of brass, and the hook of the door was of gold. In the halls were golden figures of animals, and of men who held in their hands lighted torches. Outside the courtyard was a great garden filled with blossoming pear-trees and pomegranates, and apple-trees with shining fruit, and figs, and olives. All the year round there was fruit in that garden. There were grapes in blossom, and grapes purple and ready to eat, and there were great masses of snowy pear-blossom, and pink apple-blossom, and golden ripe pears, and rosy apples.

At all of those wonders Odysseus stood and gazed, but it was not for long; for he hastened through the halls to where the queen sat in the firelight, spinning her purple yarn. He fell at her knees, and silence came on all those in the room when they looked at him, so brave and so handsome did he seem.

"Through many and great troubles have I come hither, queen," said he; "speed, I pray you, my parting right quickly, that I may come to mine own country. Too long have I suffered great sorrows far away from my own friends."

Then he sat down amongst the ashes by the fire, and for a little space no one spoke.

At last a wise old courtier said to the king: "Truly it is not right that this stranger should sit in the ashes by the fire. Bid him arise, and give him meat and drink."

At this the king took Odysseus by the hand and asked him to rise. He made one of his sons give up his silver inlaid chair, and bade his servants fetch a silver basin and a golden ewer that Odysseus might wash his hands. All kinds of dainties to eat and drink he also made them fetch, and the lords and the courtiers who were there feasted along with Odysseus, until it was time for them to go to their own homes.

Before they went the king promised Odysseus a safe convoy back to his own land.

When he was left alone with the king and queen, the queen said to him: "Tell us who thou art. I myself made the clothing that thou wearest. From whence didst thou get it?"

Then Odysseus told her of his imprisonment in the island of Calypso, of his escape, of the terrible storm that shattered his raft, and of how at length he reached the shore and met with Nausicaa.

"It was wrong of my daughter not to bring thee to the palace when she came with her maids," said the king.

But Odysseus told him why it was that Nausicaa had bade him stay behind.

"Be not vexed with this blameless maiden," he said. "Truly she is the sweetest and the fairest maid I ever saw."

Then Odysseus went to the bed that the servants had prepared for him. They had spread fair purple blankets over it, and when it was ready they stood beside it with their torches blazing, golden and red.

"Up now, stranger, get thee to sleep," said they. "Thy bed is made."

Sleep was very sweet to Odysseus that night as he lay in the soft bed with warm blankets over him. He was no longer tossed and beaten by angry seas, no longer wet and cold and hungry. The roar of furious waves did not beat in his ears, for all was still in the great halls where the flickering firelight played on the frieze of blue, and turned the brass walls into gold.

Next day the king gave a great entertainment for Odysseus. There were boxing and wrestling and leaping and running, and in all of these the brothers of Nausicaa were better than all others who tried.

But when they came to throw the weight, and begged Odysseus to try, he cast a stone heavier than all the others, far beyond where the Phæacians had thrown.

That night there was feasting in the royal halls, and the king's minstrels played and sang songs of the taking of Troy, and of the bravery of the great Odysseus. And Odysseus listened until his heart could bear no more, and tears trickled down his cheeks. Only the king saw him weep. He wondered much why Odysseus wept, and at last he asked him.

So Odysseus told the king his name, and the whole story of his adventures since he had sailed away from Troyland.

Then the king and queen and their courtiers gave rich gifts to Odysseus. A beautiful silver-studded sword was the king's gift to him.

Nausicaa gave him nothing, but she stood and gazed at him in his purple robes and felt more sure than ever that he was the handsomest and the greatest hero she had ever seen.

"Farewell, stranger," she said to him when the hour came for her to go to bed, for she knew she would not see him on the morrow. "Farewell, stranger. Sometimes think of me when thou art in thine own land."

Then said Odysseus: "All the days of my life I shall remember thee, Nausicaa, for thou hast given me my life."

Next day a company of the Phæacians went down to a ship that lay by the seashore, and with them went Odysseus. They carried the treasures that had been given to him and put them on board, and spread a rug on the deck for him. There Odysseus lay down, and as soon as the splash of the oars in the water and the rush and gush of the water from the bow of the boat told him that the ship was sailing speedily to his dear land of Ithaca, he fell into a sound sleep. Onward went the ship, so swiftly that not even a hawk flying after its prey could have kept pace with her. When the bright morning stars arose, they were close to Ithaca. The sailors quickly ran their vessel ashore and gently carried the sleeping Odysseus, wrapped round in his rug of bright purple, to where a great olive-tree bent its grey leaves over the sand. They laid him under the tree, put his treasures beside him, and left him, still heavy with slumber. Then they climbed into their ship and sailed away.

While Odysseus slept the goddess Athene shed a thick mist round him. When he awoke, the sheltering heavens, the long paths, and the trees in bloom all looked strange to him when seen through the greyness of the mist.

"Woe is me!" he groaned. "The Phæacians promised to bring me to Ithaca, but they have brought me to a land of strangers, who will surely attack me and steal my treasures."

But while he was wondering what he should do, the goddess Athene came to him. She was tall and fair and noble to look upon, and she smiled upon Odysseus with her kind grey eyes.

Under the olive-tree she sat down beside him, and told him all that had happened in Ithaca while he was away, and all that he must do to win back his kingdom and his queen.

Chapter VII
What Happened in Ithaca While Odysseus was Away

While Odysseus was fighting far away in Troyland, his baby son grew to be a big boy. And when years passed and Odysseus did not return, the boy, Telemachus, grew to be a man.

Telemachus loved his beautiful mother, Penelope, but his heart always longed for the hero father whom he could only dimly remember. As time went on, he longed more and more, for evil things came to pass in the kingdom of Odysseus.

The chiefs and lords of Ithaca admired Penelope for her beauty. They also coveted her money and her lands, and when Odysseus did not return, each one of these greedy and wicked men wished to marry her and make all that had belonged to brave Odysseus his own.

"Odysseus is surely dead," they said, "and Telemachus is only a lad and cannot harm us."

So they came to the palace where Penelope and Telemachus lived, and there they stayed, year in, year out, feasting and drinking and wasting the goods of Odysseus. Their roughness and greed troubled Penelope, but still more did they each one daily torment her by rudely asking: "Wilt thou marry me?"

At last she fell on a plan to stop them from talking to her of marriage. In the palace hall she set up a great web, beautiful and fine of woof.

Then she said, "When I have finished weaving this robe I shall give you my answer."

Each day she worked at it, but each night, when the wooers slept, she undid all that she had done during the day. So it seemed to the wooers as if the robe would never be finished.

Penelope's heart was heavy, and heavy, too, was the heart of Telemachus. For three weary years, while Odysseus was imprisoned on the island of Calypso, the mother and son pined together.

One day Telemachus sat at the door of the palace sadly watching the wooers as they drank and revelled. He was thinking of the brave father that he feared was dead, when there walked up to the door of the courtyard a stranger dressed like a warrior from another land.

The stranger was the goddess Athene. At the same time that she gained leave from the gods to set Odysseus free, they had agreed that she should go to Ithaca and help Telemachus. But she came dressed as a warrior, and not as a beautiful, grey-eyed, golden-haired goddess with golden sandals on her feet.

Telemachus rose up and shook her kindly by the hand, and led her into the hall. He took from her the heavy bronze spear that she carried, and made her sit down on one of the finest of the chairs, in a place where the noise of the rough wooers should not disturb her.

"Welcome, stranger," he said. "When thou hast had food, then shalt thou tell us in what way we can help thee."

He then made servants bring a silver basin and golden ewer that she might wash her hands, and he fetched her food and wine of the best. Soon the wooers entered, and noisily ate they and drank, and roughly they jested. Telemachus watched them and listened with an angry heart. Then, in a low voice, he said to Athene:

"These men greedily eat and drink and waste my father's goods. They think the bones of Odysseus bleach out in the rain in a far land, or are tossed about by the sea. But did my father still live, and were he to come home, the cowards would flee before him. Tell me, stranger, hast thou come from a far-off country? Hast thou ever seen my father?"

Athene answered: "Odysseus still lives. He is a prisoner on a sea-girt island, but it will not be long ere he escapes and comes home. Thou art like Odysseus, my son. Thou hast a head like his, and the same beautiful eyes."

When Athene spoke to him so kindly and so hopefully, Telemachus told her all that was in his heart. And when the wickedness and greed of the wooers was made known to her, Athene grew very angry.

"Thou art in sore need of Odysseus," she said. "If Odysseus were to come to the door now with lance in hand, soon would he scatter those shameless ones before him."

Then she told Telemachus what he must do.

"Tomorrow," said she, "call thy lords to a council meeting, and tell the wooers to return to their homes."

For himself, she told him to fit out a ship with twenty oarsmen, that he might sail to a land where he should get tidings of his father.

"Thou art tall and handsome, my friend," she said. "Be brave, that even in days to come men may praise thy name."

"Thou speakest as a father to a son. I will never forget what thou hast said," said Telemachus.

He begged Athene to stay longer, and wished to give her a costly gift. But she would not stay, nor accept any present. To Telemachus she had given a gift, though he did not know it. For into his heart she had put strength and courage, so that when she flew away like a beautiful bird across the sea she left behind her, not a frightened, unhappy boy, but a strong, brave man.

The wooers took no notice of the comings and goings of the strange warrior, so busy were they with their noisy feast. As they feasted a minstrel played to them on his lyre, and sang a song of the return of the warriors from Troyland when the fighting was over.

From her room above, Penelope heard the song, and came down. For a little, standing by the door, she listened. Then she could bear it no longer, and, weeping, she said to the minstrel:

"Sing some other song, and do not sing a song of return from Troyland to me, whose husband never returned."

Then Telemachus, in a new and manly way that made her wonder, spoke to his mother.

"Blame not the minstrel, dear mother," he said. "It is not his fault that he sings sad songs, but the fault of the gods who allow sad things to be. Thou art not the only one who hast lost a loved one in Troyland. Go back to thy room, and let me order what shall be, for I am now the head of the house."

In the same fearless, manly way he spoke to the wooers:

"Ye may feast tonight," he said; "only let there be no brawling. Tomorrow meet with me. For once and for all it must be decided if ye are to go on wasting my goods, or if I am to be master of my own house and king in mine own land."

The wooers bit their lips with rage, and some of them answered him rudely; but Telemachus paid no heed, and when at last they returned to their houses, he went upstairs to his own room. The old woman who had nursed him when he was a child carried torches before him to show him the way. When he sat down on his bed and took off his doublet, she folded the doublet and smoothed it and hung it up. Then she shut the door with its silver handle, and left Telemachus, wrapped in a soft fleece of wool, thinking far into the night of all that Athene had said to him.

When day dawned he dressed and buckled on his sword, and told heralds to call the lords to a council meeting. When all were assembled he went into the hall. In his hand he carried a bronze spear, and two of his hounds followed him, and when he went up to his father's seat and sat down there, the oldest men gave place to him. For Athene had shed on him such a wondrous grace that he looked like a young god.

"Never since brave Odysseus sailed away to Troyland have we had a council meeting," said one old lord. "I think the man who hath called this meeting is a true man—good luck go with him! May the gods give him his heart's desire."

So good a beginning did this seem that Telemachus was glad, and, burning to say all that had been in his heart for so long, he rose to his feet and spoke.

Of the loss of his father he spoke sadly, and then, with burning words, of the cowardly wooers, of their feastings and revellings and wasting of his goods, and of their insolence to Penelope and himself.

When he had thus spoken in rage and grief, he burst into tears.

For a little there was silence, then one of the wooers said angrily:

"Penelope is to blame, and no other. For three years she has deceived us. 'I will give you my answer when I have finished weaving this robe,' she said, and so we waited and waited. But now that three years have gone and a fourth has begun, it is told us by one of her maids that each night she has undone all that she has woven during the day. She can deceive us no longer. She must now finish the robe, and tell us whom she will marry. For we will not leave this place until she has chosen a husband."

Then, once again, with pleading words, Telemachus tried to move the hearts of the wooers. "If ye will not go," at last he said, "I will ask the gods to reward you for your wickedness."

As he spoke, two eagles flew, fleet as the wind, from the mountain crest. Side by side they flew until they were above the place of the council meeting. Then they wheeled about, darted with fury at each other, and tore with their savage talons at each other's heads and necks. Flapping their great wings, they then went swiftly away and were lost in the far distance.

Said a wise old man: "It is an omen. Odysseus will return, and woe will come upon the wooers. Let us make an end of these evil doings and keep harm away from us."

"Go home, old man," angrily mocked the wooers. "Prophesy to thine own children. Odysseus is dead. Would that thou hadst died with him. Then thou couldst not have babbled nonsense, and tried to hound on Telemachus in the hope that he may give thee a gift."

To Telemachus they said again:

"We will go on wasting thy goods until Penelope weds one of us."

Only one other beside the old man was brave enough to speak for Telemachus. Fearlessly and nobly did his friend Mentor blame the wooers for their shamelessness. But they jeered at him, and laughed aloud when Telemachus told them he was going to take a ship and go to look for his father.

"He will never come back," said one, "and even were Odysseus himself to return, we should slay him when he came."

Then the council meeting broke up, and the wooers went again to revel in the palace of Odysseus.

Down to the seashore went Telemachus, and knelt where the grey water broke in little white wavelets on the sand.

"Hear me," he cried, "thou who didst speak with me yesterday. I know now that thou art a god. Tell me, I pray thee, how shall I find a ship to sail across the misty sea and find my father? For there is none to help me."

Swiftly, in answer to his cry, came Athene.

"Be brave. Be thy father's son," she said. "Go back to thy house and get ready corn and wine for the voyage. I will choose the best of all the ships in Ithaca for thee, and have her launched, and manned by a crew, all of them willing men."

Then Telemachus returned to the palace. In the courtyard the wooers were slaying goats and singeing swine and making ready a great feast.

"Here comes Telemachus, who is planning to destroy us," they mocked. "Telemachus, who speaks so proudly—angry Telemachus."

Said one youth:

"Who knows but what if he goes on a voyage he will be like Odysseus, and never return. Then will we have all his riches to divide amongst ourselves, and his house will belong to the man who weds Penelope."

Telemachus knelt where the grey water broke on the sand.

Telemachus shook off the jeering crowd, and went down to the vaulted chamber where his father's treasures were kept. Gold and bronze lay there in piles, and there were great boxes of splendid clothes, and casks of wine. The heavy folding doors of the treasure chamber were shut day and night, and the old nurse was the keeper of the treasures.

Telemachus bade her get ready corn and wine for the voyage.

"When my mother has gone to rest I will take them away," he said, "for this night I go to seek my father across the sea."

At this the old nurse began to cry.

"Do not go, dear child," she wailed. "Thou art our only one, and we love thee so well. Odysseus is dead, and what canst thou do, sailing far away across the deep sea? As soon as thou art gone, those wicked men will begin to plot evil against thee. Do not go. Do not go. There is no need for thee to risk thy life on the sea and go wandering far from home."

"Take heart, nurse," said Telemachus. "The goddess Athene has told me to go, so all will be well. But promise me not to tell my dear mother that I am gone until she misses me. For I do not wish to mar her fair face with tears." The nurse promised, and began to make ready all that Telemachus wished.

Meantime Athene, in the likeness of Telemachus, found a swift-sailing ship, and men to sail it. When darkness fell, she sent sleep on the wooers and led Telemachus down to the shore where his men sat by their oars.

To the palace, where everyone slept and all was still and quiet, Telemachus brought his men. None but the old nurse knew he was going away, but they found the food and wine that she had got ready and carried it down to the ship. Then Athene went on board, and Telemachus sat beside her. A fresh west wind filled the sails and went singing over the waves. The dark water surged up at the bow as the ship cut through it. And all night long and till the dawn, the ship sailed happily on her way.

At sunrise they came to land, and Athene and Telemachus went on shore. The rulers of the country welcomed them and treated them well, but could tell nothing of Odysseus after the siege of Troy was over. Athene gave Telemachus into their care, then, turning herself into a sea-eagle, she flew swiftly away, leaving them amazed because they knew she must be one of the gods.

While Telemachus sought for news of his father in this kingdom, and the kingdoms near it, the wooers began to miss him at their feasts. They fancied he was away hunting, until, one day, as they played games in front of the palace, the man whose ship Athene had borrowed came to them.

"When will Telemachus return with my ship?" he asked. "I need it that I may cross over to where I keep my horses. I wish to catch one and break him in."

When the wooers heard from him that Telemachus had sailed away with twenty brave youths, in the swiftest ship in Ithaca, they were filled with rage.

At once they got a ship and sailed to where they might meet Telemachus in a strait between Ithaca and another rocky island.

"We will slay him there," said they. "We will give him a woeful end to his voyage in search of his father."

When Penelope heard this, and knew that her son was perhaps sailing to his doom, her heart well-nigh broke. She wept bitterly, and reproached her maidens with not having told her that Telemachus had gone.

"Slay me if thou wilt," said the old nurse, "but I alone knew it. Telemachus made me promise not to tell thee, that thy fair face might not be marred by weeping. Do not fear, the goddess Athene will take care of him."

Thus she comforted her mistress, and although she lay long awake that night, Penelope fell asleep at last. In her dreams Athene came to her and told her that Telemachus would come safely home, and so Penelope's sad heart was cheered.

While she slept the wooers sailed away in a swift, black ship, with spears in their hands and murder in their hearts. On a little rocky isle they landed until the ship of Telemachus should pass, and there they waited, that they might slay him when he came.

Chapter VIII
How Odysseus Came Home

While yet Telemachus sought news of his father, Odysseus was well-nigh home. On that misty morning when he found himself in Ithaca, and did not know it, because the grey fog made everything seem strange and unfriendly, Odysseus was very sad as he sat beside the moaning sea.

Then came Athene, and drove the mist before her, and Odysseus saw again the land that he loved, and knew that his wanderings were past. She told him the tale of the wooers, and of the unhappiness of Penelope and Telemachus, and the heart of Odysseus grew hot within him. "Stand by me!" he said to the goddess. "If thou of thy grace wilt help me, I myself will fight three hundred men."

"Truly I will stand by thee," said Athene, "and many of the greedy wooers shall stain the earth with their blood."

She then told Odysseus how the wooers were to be destroyed, and Odysseus gladly agreed to her plans. First she made him hide far in the darkness of the cave, under the olive-tree, all the gold and bronze ornaments and beautiful clothes that had been given to him in the land of Nausicaa.

Then she touched him with her golden wand. In a moment his yellow hair fell off his head; his bright eyes were dim; his skin was withered and wrinkled, and he had a stooping back and tottering legs like a feeble old man. His clothes of purple and silver she changed into torn and filthy old rags, and over his shoulders she threw the old skin of a stag with the hair worn off.

"Go now," said Athene, "to where thy faithful swineherd sits on the hill, watching his swine as they grub amongst the acorns and drink of the clear spring. He has always been true to thee and to thy wife and son. Stay with him and hear all that he has to tell, and I will go and fetch home Telemachus."

"When thou didst know all, why didst thou not tell Telemachus?" asked Odysseus. "Is he, too, to go wandering over stormy seas, far from his own land?"

"Telemachus will be a braver man for what he has gone through," said Athene. "No harm shall come to him, although the wooers in their black ship wait to slay him."

Then Athene flew across the sea, and Odysseus climbed up a rough track through the woods to where the swineherd had built himself a hut. The hut was made of stones and thorn branches, and beside it were sties for the swine made in the same way. The wooers had eaten many swine at their daily feasts, but thousands remained. These the swineherd tended, with three men and four fierce dogs to help him.

At an open space on the hill, from whence he could look down at the woods and the sea, Odysseus found the swineherd sitting at the door of his hut making himself a pair of sandals out of a brown ox-hide.

When the swineherd's dogs saw a dirty, bent old man toiling up the hill, they rushed at him, barking furiously. Up they leapt on him and would have torn him to pieces if their master had not cast away his ox-hide, dashed after them, scolded them and beaten them, and then driven them off with showers of stones.

"If my dogs had killed thee I should have been forever ashamed," he said to Odysseus, "and without that I have enough sorrow. For while my noble master may be wandering in a strange land and lacking food, I have to feed his fat swine for others to eat."

So speaking, he led Odysseus to his hut. He laid some brushwood on the floor, spread over it the soft, shaggy skin of a wild goat, and bade Odysseus be seated. Then he went out to the sties, killed two sucking pigs, and roasted them daintily. When they were ready he cut off the choicest bits and gave them to Odysseus, with a bowl of honey-sweet wine.

While Odysseus ate and drank, the swineherd talked to him of the greed and wastefulness of the wooers, and in silence Odysseus listened, planning in his heart how he might punish them.

"Tell me thy master's name," he said at length. "I have travelled in many lands. Perchance I may have seen him, and may give thee news of him."

But the swineherd answered: "Each vagrant who comes straying to the land of Ithaca goes to my mistress with lying tales of how he has seen or heard of my master. She receives them all kindly, and asks many questions, while tears run down her cheeks. You, too, old

Odysseus looked down at the woods and the sea.

man, would quickly make up a story if anyone would give thee some new clothes. My master is surely dead, and wherever I may go I shall never again find a lord so gentle."

Then said Odysseus: "My friend, I swear to thee that Odysseus shall return. In this year, as the old moon wanes and the new is born, he shall return to his home."

When the other herds returned that evening they found Odysseus and their master still deep in talk. At night the swineherd made a feast of the best that he had, and still they talked, almost until dawn. The night was black and stormy, and a drenching rain blotted out the moon, but the swineherd, leaving Odysseus lying in the bed he had made for him, with his own thick mantle spread over him, went outside and lay under a rock that sheltered him from the storm, keeping guard on the white-tusked boars that slept around him. And Odysseus knew that he had still at least one servant who was faithful and true.

While Odysseus dwelt with the swineherd, Athene sought Telemachus and bade him hasten home. Speedily Telemachus went back to his ship and his men. The hawsers were loosed, the white sail hauled up, and Athene sent a fresh breeze that made the ship cut through the water like a white-winged bird. It was night when they passed the island where the wooers awaited their coming, and in the darkness none saw them go by.

By daybreak they reached Ithaca, and Telemachus, as Athene had bidden him, sent on the men to the harbour with the ship, but made them put him ashore on the woody coast near the swineherd's dwelling.

With his bronze-shod spear in his hand, Telemachus strode up the rocky path. Odysseus and the swineherd had kindled a fire, and were preparing the morning meal, when Odysseus heard the noise of footsteps. He looked out and saw a tall lad with yellow hair and bright eyes, and a fearless, noble face. "Surely here is a friend," he said to the swineherd. "Thy dogs are not barking, but jump up and fawn on him."

The swineherd looked, and when he saw his young master he wept for joy.

"I thought I should never see thee more, sweet light of my eyes," he said. "Come into my hut, that I may gladden my heart with the sight of thee."

He then spread before him the best he had, and the three men ate together. Although Odysseus seemed only a poor, ragged, old beggar, Telemachus treated him with such gentleness and such courtesy that Odysseus was proud and glad of his noble son. Soon Telemachus sent the swineherd to tell Penelope of his safe return, and while he was gone Athene entered the hut. She made herself invisible to Telemachus, but beckoned to Odysseus to go outside.

"The time is come for thee to tell thy son who thou art," she said, and touched him with her golden wand.

At once Odysseus was again a strong man, dressed in fine robes, and radiant and beautiful as the sun.

When he went back into the hut Telemachus thought he was a god.

"No god am I," said Odysseus; "I am thy father, Telemachus."

And Odysseus took his son in his arms and kissed him, and the tears that he had kept back until now ran down his cheeks. Telemachus flung his arms round his father's neck, and he, too, wept like a little child, so glad was he that Odysseus had come home.

All day they spoke of the wooers and plotted how to slay them.

When the swineherd returned, and Athene had once more changed Odysseus into an old beggar-man, he told Telemachus that the wooers had returned, and were so furious with Telemachus for escaping from them, that they were going to kill him next day.

At this Telemachus smiled to his father, but neither said a word.

Next morning Telemachus took his spear and said to the swineherd:

"I go to the palace to see my mother. As for this old beggar-man, lead him to the city, that he may beg there."

And Odysseus, still pretending to be a beggar, said:

"It is better to beg in the town than in the fields. My garments are very poor and thin, and this frosty air chills me; but as soon as I am warmed at the fire and the sun grows hot, I will gladly set out."

Down the hill to the city strode Telemachus. When he came to the palace, his old nurse, whom he found busy in the hall, wept for joy. And when Penelope heard his voice, she came from her room and cast her arms round him and kissed his face and his eyes, and said, while tears ran down her cheeks:

"Thou art come, sweet light of my eyes. I thought I should never see thee more."

Then Telemachus, looking like a young god, with his spear in his hand and his two hounds following at his heels, went to the hall where the wooers sat. To his friend Mentor he told his adventures, but he looked on the wooers with silence and scorn.

Soon Odysseus and the swineherd followed him to the city. A beggar's bag, all tattered, was slung round the shoulders of Odysseus. In his hand he carried a staff. Men who saw him, tattered and feeble, mocked at him and his guide. But Odysseus kept down the anger in his heart, and they went on to the palace. Near the doorway, lying in the dirt, thin and old and rough of coat, lay Argos, the dog that long ago had been the best and fleetest that had hunted the hares and deer with Odysseus.

When he heard his master's voice he wagged his tail and tried to crawl near him. But he was too feeble to move. He could only look up with loving, wistful eyes that were almost blind, and thump his tail gladly. So glad was he that his faithful heart broke for joy, and before Odysseus could pat his head or speak a kind word to him, old Argos rolled over dead.

There were tears in the eyes of Odysseus as he walked past the body of his friend. He sat down on the threshold leaning on his staff, and when Telemachus sent him bread and meat from his table he ate hungrily. When the meal was over he went round the hall begging from the wooers. Some gave him scraps of broken meats, others called him hard names and bade him begone, and one of them seized a footstool and struck him with it.

But Odysseus still kept down the anger in his heart, and went back to his seat on the threshold with his beggar's bag full of the scraps that had been given to him.

As he sat there, a common beggar, well known for his greed and impudence, came to the palace.

"Get thee hence, old man," said he to Odysseus, "else I shall knock all thy teeth from thy head."

More, too, he said, rudely and roughly, and at last he struck Odysseus.

Then Odysseus could bear no more, and smote him such a blow on his neck that the bones were broken, and he fell on the ground with blood gushing from his mouth. Odysseus dragged him outside by the heels, and propped him, with his staff in his hands, against the courtyard wall.

"Sit there," he said, "and scare off dogs and swine." The wooers laughed and enjoyed the sport, and gave gifts of food to the sturdy old beggar, as they took Odysseus to be. All evening they feasted and drank, but when night fell they went to their own homes.

When they were gone Odysseus and Telemachus carried all the helmets and swords and sharp-pointed spears that stood in the hall away to the armoury and hid them there.

Then Telemachus went to his room to rest, but Odysseus sat in the hall where the servants were clearing away the remains of the feast. While he sat there, Penelope came with her maids and rested on a chair in front of the glowing wood fire on which the servants had piled fresh logs.

She talked kindly and gently to the old beggar-man, and bade the old nurse bring water to wash his weary feet.

Now, once long ago, a wild boar that he hunted had torn the leg of Odysseus with his tusk, and as the old nurse washed his feet she saw the scar. In a moment she knew her master, and cried out. The brazen bath fell with a clang on the floor, and the water was spilt.

"Thou art Odysseus," she said; "I did not know thee, my dear child, until I found the scar."

Penelope must have heard her glad cry, had not Athene at that moment made her deep in thoughts of other things. Quickly Odysseus bade the old nurse be silent, and the old woman obeyed him.

Before Penelope went to rest she said sadly to Odysseus: "I feel that the end is drawing near. Soon I shall be parted from the house of Odysseus. My husband, who was always the best and bravest, used to set up the twelve axes ye see standing here, and between each axe he shot an arrow. I have told the wooers that I shall marry whichever one of them can do the like. Then I shall leave this house, which must be forever most dear to me."

Then answered the old beggar-man: "Odysseus will be here when they shoot. It will be Odysseus who shoots between the axes."

Penelope, longing for his words to be true, went up to her room and lay crying on her bed until her pillows were wet. Then Athene sent sleep upon her eyelids and made her forget all her sorrows.

Odysseus, too, would have tossed all night wide awake, with a heart full of anger and revenge, had not Athene gently laid her hands on his eyes and made him fall asleep.

Next day the wooers came to the palace, and with rough jest and rude word they greeted Odysseus.

"Who harms this man must fight with me," said Telemachus, and at that the wooers shouted with laughter.

But a stranger who sat amongst them cried out in a voice of fear:

"I see your hands and knees shrouded in blackness! I see your cheeks wet with tears! The walls and the pillars drip blood; the porch is full of shadows, and pale ghosts are hastening out of the grey mist that fills the palace."

At this the wooers laughed the more, for they thought the man was mad. But, as in a dream, he had seen truly what was to come to pass.

Weeping, Penelope then brought forth from the armoury the great bow with which Odysseus had shot in years that were past. Her heart was full of love for Odysseus, and she could not bear to wed another.

Telemachus then threw aside his red cloak and ranged out the bronze axes.

One by one the wooers tried to move the great bow and make it drive a swift arrow before it. One by one they failed.

And when it seemed as if no man there was strong enough to move it, Odysseus took it in his hands, and between each axe he shot an arrow. When the last arrow was shot he tore off his rags, and in a voice that rang through the palace he cried to Telemachus: "Now is it time to prepare supper for the wooers! Now, at last, is this terrible trial ended. I go to shoot at another mark!"

With that he shot an arrow at the wooer who had ever been the most insolent and the most cruel. It smote him in the throat, his blood dripped red on the ground, and he fell dead.

The others gave a great cry of rage, but Odysseus looked at them with burning eyes, and with a voice that made them tremble he cried:

"Ye dogs! ye said I should never return, and, like the traitors ye are, ye have wasted my goods and insulted my queen. But now death has come for you, and none shall escape."

In vain did the cowards, their faces pale with fear, beg for mercy. Mercy there was none that day. It was useless for those who drew their swords and rushed on Odysseus to try to slay him, for ere their swords could touch him, his bow had driven sharp arrows into their hearts.

One of the servants of the palace treacherously climbed into the armoury and brought spears and shields and helmets for the wooers. But even that did not daunt Odysseus and his son. Telemachus, with his spear, slew man after man. When his arrows were done Odysseus also snatched a spear, and they fought side by side. Beside them fought the swineherd and one other man, and they all fought the more fearlessly because, all the time, Athene put fresh courage in their hearts.

There were four men to very many others when that fight began. When it was ended the floor ran with blood, and Odysseus, like a lion at bay, stood with the dead bodies of the wooers piled in heaps around him and his face and hands stained with blood.

When all lay dead, the old nurse gave a great cry of joy.

"Rejoice in thy heart, old nurse," said Odysseus. "It is an unholy thing to rejoice over slain men."

The nurse hastened to Penelope's room.

"Penelope, dear child!" she cried, "Odysseus is come home, and all the wooers lie dead."

At first Penelope would not believe her. Too good did it seem to be true. Even when she came down and saw Odysseus leaning against a tall pillar in the light of the fire, she would not believe what her own eyes saw.

"Surely, mother, thy heart is as hard as stone," said Telemachus. "Dost thou not know my father?"

But Penelope saw only a ragged beggar-man, soiled with the blood of the men he had slain, old and ugly and poor.

Then Athene shed her grace upon Odysseus, and once more he was tall and strong and gallant to look upon, with golden hair curling like hyacinth flowers around his head. And Penelope ran to him and threw out her arms, and they held each other close and wept together like those who have suffered shipwreck, and have been tossed for long by angry seas, and yet have won safely home at last.

And when the sun went down that night on the little rocky island of Ithaca in the far seas, the heart of Odysseus was glad, for he knew that his wanderings were ended.

Lightning Source UK Ltd.
Milton Keynes UK
UKHW021514250321
380978UK00008B/1471

9 781389 673818